THE MONEY SAVVY KID$™ CLUB

Garage Sale Riches

Volume One

By Susan Beacham & Lynnette Khalfani-Cox

Illustrations by Tom Deja

Dedication

This book is dedicated to my loving husband Earl,
and to our three wonderful children, Aziza, Jakada and Alexis.
-Lynnette

Special Thanks

The authors wish to thank the following people for their brilliance and devotion

Illustrator: Tom Deja
Cover Design: Mary Jo Cadiz
Editor: Cindy Richards
Poet: Michael Beacham

Publisher Cataloging-In-Publication data:
Beacham, Susan.
Garage sale riches/ by Susan Beacham and Lynnette Khalfani-Cox ; illustrations by Tom Deja.
SUMMARY: Four children have to decide what to do with the money they raise from a garage sale. Intended to help young people understand the importance of proper money management.
p. cm. – (The money savvy kids club)
ISBN 978-0-9842139-0-0
1. Money–Juvenile fiction. 2. Helping behavior in children–Juvenile fiction.
I. Khalfani-Cox, Lynnette. II. Deja, Tom (ill.). III. Title. IV. Series.
PZ7 .B3541 Ga 2009
813–dc22
LCCN# 2009935974
2nd edition

It was Saturday morning and Isaiah was busy going through box after box of stuff in his parents' garage. There was so much stuff in there that the family minivan couldn't even fit.

"What is all this junk?" he asked his mom.

"Isaiah Samuel Jones, what you call junk, I call treasures," she said.

She held up a gold-studded belt and a lacy white blouse.

"These are vintage clothes. Think of them as antiques that will make you a lot of money."

Isaiah didn't believe anybody would pay a lot of money for worn-out clothes. But his mom made money buying and selling the stuff, so he figured he could, too.

Isaiah grabbed a marker and wrote "Old Ventij Clothz" on the box.

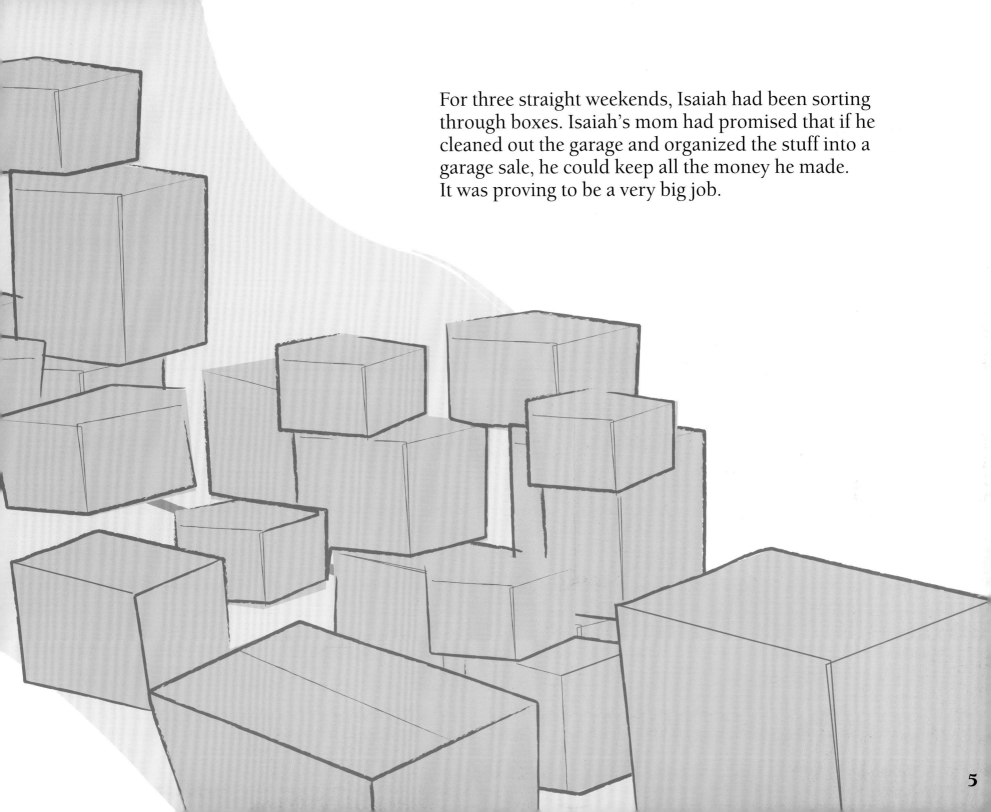

For three straight weekends, Isaiah had been sorting through boxes. Isaiah's mom had promised that if he cleaned out the garage and organized the stuff into a garage sale, he could keep all the money he made.
It was proving to be a very big job.

He had enlisted the help of his best friends, Sandy, Dennis and Stephanie. In return, he promised to split the garage sale profits with them.

Stephanie was complaining. She hated cleaning.

As usual, Isaiah had to remind her of their deal. If she helped, he would split the money with her.

"Oh, right," Stephanie said. "If we do this we'll get lots of money."

The others were more willing workers.

"I'll start sweeping," Dennis volunteered.

"I'll put all these shoes onto the shelves," Sandy offered.

"I'll keep going through these boxes," Isaiah told his friends.

"I guess I can sort these papers into neat stacks," Stephanie said.

As the kids worked, Linda
the letter carrier arrived
with the day's mail.

"Hi, Isaiah. I see you're still
cleaning the garage,"
she said.

"We should be done today,"
Isaiah answered cheerfully.

"That's what you said
last weekend," Stephanie
grumbled. "I don't think
we're ever going to finish."

"I know what you mean," Linda said. "Sometimes it seems like the piles of envelopes will never end. But I keep working and the letters disappear, one house at a time."

"Don't you get tired of working that hard?" Stephanie asked.

"Sometimes. But it's worth it. I make sure people get their mail and when I finish my work, I get paid," Linda said as she headed to her next delivery.

Isaiah squatted between two boxes and wrote something in his notebook.

For the next two hours, Isaiah and his pals kept busy in the garage. At noon, a man drove into the driveway. The man popped out of his car carrying what looked like a big suitcase.

"Hi, mister. Can I help you?" Isaiah asked.

"I'm Mr. Peterson," the man said. "I sell vacuum cleaners and I have an appointment with your mom."

"Mooooooom," Isaiah yelled, "someone's here!"

"I didn't know there were salesmen who sold vacuum cleaners," Dennis said.

"Oh sure there are," Mr. Peterson said. "There are people who sell just about anything you can think of."

Isaiah's mom opened the kitchen door and said, "Hello, Mr. Peterson. Please come in."

Then she turned to the children and said, "Why don't you kids take a break. I made you some sandwiches and there's juice in the fridge."

14

As they sat down to lunch, Isaiah walked behind the counter, pulled out his pencil and notebook again and scribbled something inside.

Stephanie took a bite of her sandwich and mumbled, "I just hope that suitcase of his doesn't end up in the garage."

As the kids put their dishes into the sink, they saw Isaiah's mom point to a shiny black vacuum cleaner and say, "This one will be perfect."

"Good choice," Mr. Peterson said as Isaiah's mom wrote a check for the vacuum cleaner.

Mr. Peterson looked at the check and smiled broadly. "Thank you very much for your business," he said.

"Keep up the good work in the garage, kids," Mr. Peterson said. "I've got to run. I still have five more families to visit. My day won't end until this evening."

"Wow. You work a lot of hours," Sandy said.

"Yes," Mr. Peterson said. "But I have a little girl and if I don't work, I can't buy her the things she needs, like food and clothing."

Isaiah ducked behind a box and pulled out his notebook once more.

As Mr. Peterson left, a neighbor named Mariah rode up on her bicycle.

Mariah was 19 years old. She attended the local college.

"Hey, Isaiah," she called. "Is your brother, James, around?"

"He's upstairs," Isaiah answered. "I'll get him."

"Jaaaaaaaammmmes!" Isaiah yelled. "Your math tutor is here!"

"What's a tutor?" Stephanie asked.

"Someone who helps you learn stuff," Isaiah replied. "My big brother may know a lot more than me since he's 12. But he doesn't know everything about math. So Mariah teaches him math."

19

"Doesn't James' teacher at school teach him math?" Sandy asked.

"Yeah, but having a tutor is like getting extra help to learn something," Isaiah answered.

"I still don't get it," Stephanie said, turning to Mariah. "Why would you spend your Saturday afternoon helping James learn math?"

"Tutoring is my job," Mariah said.

"Who is your boss?" Sandy asked.

"Yeah, and what's the name of the company you work for?" Stephanie asked.

"Actually, I work for myself. I'm an entrepreneur," Mariah said proudly.

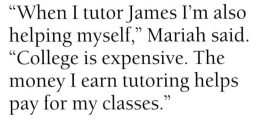

"When I tutor James I'm also helping myself," Mariah said. "College is expensive. The money I earn tutoring helps pay for my classes."

Mariah went inside and the kids went back to work. Two hours later, Mariah left the Jones house with a smile on her face and $40 in her hand.

Isaiah took out his pencil and wrote something in his notebook.

By the end of the day, Isaiah and his friends had finally finished cleaning the garage.

"We'll probably make a million dollars selling all this stuff," Isaiah said.

"After all this work, we'd better!" Stephanie said.

"Well, if we want to make a million dollars, we'd better start thinking *savvy!*" said Isaiah. "We should call ourselves The Money Savvy Kids Club."

"I like that name," Sandy said.

"I like the idea of being smart about my money," Stephanie said.

During recess on Monday, the four friends talked about what they wanted to do with the money they would make from the garage sale.

"I think I'll save my money so I can buy a new bike," Sandy said.

"I'm going to spend all my money on the Pioneer Princess DVD series. I saw them on TV," Stephanie said.

"I'm going to save my money to pay for college," Isaiah said. "How about you, Dennis?"

"Did you guys meet the new boy, Harry Winters?" Dennis asked.

"Yeah, he's kind of quiet, but he seems nice," Isaiah answered.

"I think he's sad," Dennis said. "His family lost their home in that big hurricane. I think I'll donate my money to help those hurricane families."

The garage sale was a big hit.

At the end of the day, the kids were exhausted -- until Isaiah started counting the money they had made.

"Are we millionaires?" Stephanie demanded.

"Well, we didn't quite make a million dollars," Isaiah said. "But we did earn $216. That means we each get $54."

"Sounds like I arrived just in time," Sandy's mom said as she walked into the garage. "I'm here to take you to the mall, just like I promised. But first, I brought you each a present."

She set down four piggy banks. Each one had four slots that said "save," "spend," "donate" and "invest."

"This is a special piggy bank called the 'Money Savvy Pig,'" she said. "It helps you understand that you always have four choices for your money. You can save it, spend it, donate it to a worthy cause, or invest it."

"Hey, the Money Savvy Pig sounds perfect for The Money Savvy Kids Club!" Isaiah said excitedly to Sandy's mom.

Sandy, Dennis and Isaiah thanked her. Stephanie said she was ready to go to the mall.

At Mega Mall, Stephanie went straight to the video store and bought two Pioneer Princess DVDs. Together, they cost $50. "I've been wanting these my whole life!" she said.

Sandy bought a doll that cost $15.

"Isn't she cute?" Sandy asked her friends.

Isaiah spent $5 playing video games while Dennis watched.

"I think I'll just keep my money for the hurricane families," Dennis said. All the work and shopping had made the kids really hungry. They headed to the food court, where each of them spent $4 on pizza and soda.

"Hey, I'm totally out of money," Stephanie said. "But Dennis still has almost all of his money left. That's not fair!"

"What's not fair about it?" Dennis demanded. "It's not my fault you spent all your money, Stephanie."

Sandy agreed. "Stephanie, don't you remember my mom saying we all have four choices of what to do with our money? Dennis chose to save most of his to donate it to the victims of the hurricane and you chose to spend all of yours."

"Yeah, but I just got so excited when I saw those DVDs," Stephanie grumbled. "Can't you guys share just a little of your money with me?"

All of a sudden, Isaiah bounced to his feet.

"Stephanie, here's what I'll share with you," he said. "Listen to this."

And then Isaiah began singing.

31

"It's really quite funny,

This thing called money.

If there's one thing we've learned, it's that money is earned.

Like mail lady Linda brings you mail from a sender.

Mr. P. sells vacuums to help you tidy up rooms.

And Mariah's own biz... tutoring high school kids.

And as far as I'm concerned, money's worth more when it's earned.

What was once a hodgepodge is now a clean garage.

We turned trash into treasure and this work gave us pleasure.

We sold the goods with panache, and in return earned cold hard cash.

But no matter how you make it, just be careful where you take it.

You might think it's going to last, but your money sure can go fast.

Don't spend it all right away, you'll need some for another day.

Your money may not last long, and when your money's gone, it's gone!"

"So that's what you were writing all this time in your notebook, Isaiah," Sandy said. "Now I understand what all our hard work was for."

"I think we all do," said Dennis.

"OK, guys, even I get it," Stephanie said, rolling her eyes. "We shouldn't waste our money because we have to work hard to earn it. Then we can save it, spend it or put it away for the future, right?"

"And don't forget that we can give away money, too," Dennis said.

Isaiah smiled thinking about the lessons they'd all learned. He smiled even more when he realized that his parents' junky old garage was full of riches after all.

33